ROUGH ICE

by Beman Lord

pictures by Arnold Spilka

HENRY Z. WALCK, INC.
New York

To Hamden Library, Hamden, Connecticut
for not letting me ... procrastinate

Copyright © 1963 by Beman Lord. All rights reserved. ISBN: 0-8098-2027-7. Library of Congress Catalog Card Number: 63-17190. Printed in the United States of America.

Contents

1. Predicament

As soon as Eddie entered his house, he yelled, "Hey, Mom, where are you?"

"Here," his mother called from the back bedroom. "Just lying down for a few minutes."

Eddie tossed his books on the table and ran to her room. "Mom, the Governor has called for a physical fitness program. 'Make youth stronger,' he says. The fellows and I have formed a club and they elected me president. We're going to work out as often as we can. What do you think, Mom?"

"Why I think that's fine," his mother said, as she fluffed the pillows behind her and sat up. "But I have a feeling there is something more to his and your plan."

"Well, there is one small problem," Eddie said slowly. "We're the only ones that have their cellar fixed up, and the club needs a place this winter to exercise. After all, it's for the good of the country and how can you say no to the Governor?"

"Several people have done just that, if my memory serves me correctly," she answered.

"I'm serious, Mom. How about it?"

"We'll discuss it at supper. Your father should have a say in this matter. He really did a lot of work on the cellar."

At supper that night Eddie waited until all
the plates were filled before he spoke. He
explained his plan, leaving out the part about
using the cellar.

8

"A good idea," Mr. MacDougal said. "I believe in exercise."

"Before you go too far," his mother interrupted, "there is 'one small problem.' They would like to use our cellar."

"I can't see any harm in that," his father said. "Would you please pass the butter?"

"There is if I have to feed them after a workout," she answered. "Is there any equipment involved in the program?"

"Just one or two things," Eddie said. "Bud is going to bring over his brother's old bar bells. Archie is bringing an old bike that we are going to rig up to stand still. I have to get a set of pulleys. Nothing much."

"The one or two things is now three," his mother said, trying not to smile. "My vote will be yes—but no food is to be served."

"I'll go along with your mother," his father said, "and I'll even help you get rigged up. Let's say I'm protecting my interests. I only ask that you keep the place neat."

"Thanks a million," Eddie said. "We can start tomorrow. What's for dessert?"

"Didn't the Governor say anything about sweets?" his mother asked.

After dinner his mother did the dishes,

and Eddie helped. He then went into the living room where his dad was reading the paper.

"I see by the paper that the Blues are going to have a Pee Wee Hockey League again this winter at the arena. Tryouts are next Saturday," his dad said.

Eddie didn't say anything as he walked over to a chair and sat down.

"Are you going to try out?"

Eddie hadn't been able to try out the year before. He had been in bed with the measles. Bud had, and said it was lots of fun. But last winter Eddie had noticed his ankle was sort of weak when he did heavy skating. Every once in a while it would "break." Eddie wanted to try out; but what if he didn't make it? His father sure would be disappointed in him. Mr. MacDougal had been the Blues' star wing for years. "Sure," he said, confidently—or so he hoped, "nothing tried, nothing gained."

"I believe the saying is nothing ventured, nothing gained," his father replied, with a smile. "Your vocabulary is going to be the death of all of us."

"I like words. When I'm excited I forget

the better ones, but they are . . ." Eddie paused as he tried to think of just the right word. "Exotic." He smiled, pleased with himself. "How's that one, Dad?"

"Tremendous," his dad answered. "But I bet you can't spell it."

"You've got me there," Eddie answered.

"What are you trying out for?" his dad asked, as he put the paper back in the rack.

Eddie thought about all the times his father had talked about playing forward for the Blues. "Forward, of course," he said.

"Good, it will be nice to have another forward in the family," his dad said. "I'll give you a few pointers before the tryouts. I still know some of the gang down at the arena, and they might let us in for an hour or so."

"You sure must miss it, Dad."

"Hockey is for young people," his dad said. "It's a rough game, and my bones are much happier now. At least when I'm selling I don't get any body checks. Now it's only bad checks." Mr. MacDougal waited for a laugh from Eddie. There was no reaction. "Did I high-stick that one? I didn't think it was above your shoulders."

"I'll think about it," Eddie said, "but it may be out of my league. You're too cool for me."

"Settle down, you're getting out of *my* league with that kind of talk," his dad said, as he pulled himself up from his chair. "I'll call the arena and see if we can use the ice." He went to telephone.

Eddie picked up the newspaper and turned to the sports page. The announcement said that fifteen boys would be picked for each team, and there would be four teams. Sixty boys all together. "Holy smoke," Eddie thought, "Bud said last year over a hundred tried out. Am I good enough?"

"We can use the ice at seven o'clock tomorrow morning," his dad said, as he came back into the living room. "That will mean getting up at six. But if you make the team that's what you'll have to do anyway. Do you think you can pull yourself out of bed by that hour?"

"It will be a strain—especially on a Saturday," Eddie said. "But well worth it. Maybe we can work on the cellar when we get back."

"Come on. Let's get our skates and go downstairs. If you're going to play forward, they should be razor sharp."

After the skates had been filed, Eddie called his friends and told them to come over around ten o'clock. Then he went to his room. He lay down on the bed and tried to read, but couldn't concentrate on what he was reading. What if he didn't make forward? Out of a hundred boys did he have a chance? What a predicament for a fellow who had a father who broke all scoring records for the Blues and still held the record!

2. Catastrophe

They were at the players' entrance at 6:45 and a watchman let them in. "It's good to see you again, Rocket, after all these years. So this is your boy. Let's hope he's going to follow in your skates. The Blues sure could use a good scoring wing. I'll turn on a few lights and just make yourself to home. Sorry I can't stay to watch."

The arena looked so big and quiet without any people. "It's overpowering," Eddie thought to himself. That was a good word, but he wasn't going to say it out loud.

"The first thing we'll do is warm up," his dad said, after they had put on their skates. "Take it easy at first. Remember to push from the side with each foot. Keep the other one straight. That's how you're going to get the power. When you want to pick up speed, keep your feet closer together and push more often."

Eddie tried to grasp everything his father said. In his eagerness, he tried too hard and went sprawling.

"Settle down," his dad said. "It won't come in a minute. Just skate slowly around the rink a few times. Give your legs a chance to get used to the movement again." After

they had done this several times, Mr. Mac-
Dougal started to pick up speed. He moved

beautifully around the ice. Eddie tried to follow him. "Feet close together and push at shorter intervals," he told himself. He managed to pick up a little speed. "I've got the idea," he thought. Within a few minutes his right ankle suddenly gave way and sent him to the ice.

His dad didn't say anything, but waited for Eddie to pick himself up and start again. Halfway around, the ankle turned again. He regained his balance and didn't fall. Fortunately his dad didn't see this; but Eddie realized that every time he pushed too hard the ankle gave him trouble. It was still weak, and he would have to baby it.

"Are you ready for a little stickwork?" his dad called over his shoulder.

"Fine," Eddie said. "I'll take right wing."

They moved down the ice slowly as they passed the puck back and forth. "Keep it coming in front of me," his dad yelled, "and snap those wrists a little quicker. That will move the puck faster."

Eddie's head was buzzing from all the advice his dad was giving.

"You're doing fine," his dad called, but Eddie didn't believe him. They tried the figure eight down and back. "This weave is very important. It makes it harder for the other team to stop you and is the setup for the passing and scoring. Speed it up," his dad said.

Before they reached the center line, Eddie had fallen. His dad skated over to him. "You okay?"

"I hit a rough piece of ice," Eddie said, as he stood up, not wanting to tell his dad the truth. He just couldn't skate fast enough, and when he tried his ankle would break. "I'll never make wing. What a catastrophe!" he thought. "Another good word gone to waste. Here I am the son of a star forward and president of a physical fitness club and a mess!"

"Let's call it a day," his dad said. "We still have the cellar to fix up." As they were driving home, his dad continued talking, "You move well, and the stickwork is fine. You just need practice. That plus a few lessons on paper. You should make forward."

"Should make forward," Eddie thought. "*Should* and *will* are two entirely different matters."

When they arrived home, Bud was waiting
for them with his brother's bar bells and an
old bike. "Archie had to go with his parents
to his grandmother's, but he left the bike. I
hear you've already had a workout. How did
it go?"

"I'll tell you about it later," Eddie said.
"Let's get this stuff down to the cellar. My
dad is going to help us get set up."

Within an hour they had the bike attached to some boards and a set of pulleys rigged up. "That should do it," Mr. MacDougal said. "I'll leave you two. I haven't had this much exercise in years. And even though it's Saturday, I have to go to the office."

Eddie got on the bike and started to pedal slowly. He wondered if the movement would strengthen his ankle.

"Why the glum face, Eddie?" Bud asked. "You look like it's the end of the world. Tell Uncle Bud your story."

"Well, it's . . . horrendous, and I . . ."

"Easy does it," Bud interrupted. "This is Bud, remember. Just use the five-cent words with me."

"I'm sorry," Eddie laughed, and then be-

came very serious. "My dad and I practiced
this morning. I'm not very good plus my
ankle keeps breaking. I'm not fast and a forward has got to be fast and my ankle I'm sure

30

won't hold when I skate fast and I've got to be forward. Maybe I should resign as president of the club. I'm not physically fit."

The words came tumbling out so fast that Bud threw his hand up and said, "Whoa there. See if I've got it straight. You have a weak ankle. Some people do, some people don't. Straps would help a little bit, but your skates are probably not fitting right. Problem 1 can be partly solved with a new pair of skates. Problem 2: Why do you have to be forward?"

"My dad was a star...."

"I know all that. But there are other spots on the team. From what I hear, more fellows are going to try out for that position than any other. Plus all of last year's forwards are coming back including myself. Why not try for defense or goalie?"

"But forward is what my dad played, and I know he'd want me to, too."

"Making the team seems more important to me. Who cares what position it is? I'd try for goalie. Your ankle would hold up because there isn't so much heavy skating. And you'd certainly see plenty of action." Bud paused and waited for an answer.

Eddie stopped pedaling while he thought. Making the team was important; but his dad sure would be disappointed if he didn't play forward. He had said it would be nice to have another forward in the family. Could he play goalie? "My dad says I move well and my stick-work is fine. But I've never played goalie."

"Nothing to it," Bud said. "All it needs is practice. I have an idea that will help us both. After lunch bring some gloves, your hockey stick, roller skates and meet me on the tennis courts. Hey, that's something. Hockey stick, roller skates and tennis in one sentence. Better bring your catcher's equipment, too."

Eddie jumped down from the bike. "Great, in fact it's ..."

"Don't waste time thinking. Just move."

Eddie moved. He grabbed a sandwich and a glass of milk, and then his equipment. By the time he reached the tennis courts, Bud had set up two cardboard boxes for goals.

"I'm just going to pretend you know nothing about goal tending," Bud said. "So we'll have a quick lesson. While I'm talking put on your skates and the chest and knee pads. The most important thing to remember is to watch the puck at all times. The whole idea is to keep it out of the goal. Your feet should stay close together so the puck won't find an opening there. You'll have a wider stick and your skates will be duller. A goalie's skates shouldn't move too fast and he doesn't really go anywhere except in the cage. Once in a great while he gets out, but we'll worry about

that when it happens. You can also use your hands. Let's see what happens."

Bud skated to the center of the court and started a slow weave toward the goal. "I won't come in too close since there will be defense men helping you," he called, and sailed the puck across the cement. Eddie easily blocked the shot with his stick and moved the puck around one of the boxes. "Good boy," Bud said.

"Just beginner's luck," Eddie replied. After blocking several more shots successfully,

Eddie said, "You know, this really is fun."

"Who said you didn't know anything about goal tending," Bud said. "You're a natural."

They played this way for the rest of the afternoon. "What we really need is another forward," Bud said, on the way home. "It would be good for my passing and also your blocking. I'll get Archie to come tomorrow. Oh, before I forget. Forget about problem 3. We've got a good president. I'll take a strong brain and a weak ankle any day."

When Eddie reached home, he suddenly thought that his dad might see him with all the equipment. He'd certainly put two and two together and not get five. Eddie checked the garage, and it was empty. Good, his dad wasn't home yet. He started down the cellar stairs as his mother opened her bedroom window. "What, no basketball?" Eddie didn't answer.

3. The Dilemma

The next week was a busy one. All the equipment in the cellar was forgotten. After school, Eddie practiced playing goalie with Bud and Archie. In the evenings his dad gave him lessons on how to play forward. Eddie still hadn't decided definitely what position he was going to try out for. A goalie certainly was important to a team and he was enjoying playing that position. Bud and Archie hadn't been able to score too many times, even at the beginning. But what about his dad? It was a . . . dilemma.

Saturday morning he was up bright and early; the tryouts started at seven. He and Bud took the bus to the arena.

"What did I tell you," Bud whispered to Eddie, as they were putting on their skates. "There must be over a hundred guys trying out."

"I've got to make it," Eddie said nervously.

"Could I have your attention, boys," an older man called. "My name is Speed Randall and I am the coach for the Blues. There will be four teams each with fifteen men and coached by members of the Blues. Names will appear in Monday's paper, and those who make it will report here the same time next

40

Saturday. All the forwards move to this side
of the rink, defense to the other side, and
goalies in the middle. Centers over here
by me."

All the boys did as they were told, and Eddie skated to the middle. He had decided to go out for goalie. Fifteen other boys had also decided on that position. "Settle down. You're a good goalie," he kept telling himself over and over.

"We'll make teams and see what you look like in action," Speed said. "We understand that you haven't been on skates for some time and are taking that into consideration."

It took most of the morning for all the teams to play. Bud managed to score one goal when his team played. He would have no trouble making a team. Eddie, when his turn came, gave up one goal but made five saves.

"How do you think we did?" Bud asked, as they rode the bus home.

"You won't have any trouble making a team. You're good. But I don't know about little old me," Eddie said. "It was fun, though."

"How did it go?" Mr. MacDougal asked, when Eddie got home.

"Fine. We'll know Monday. It will be in the paper."

"Your mother will have to give me the news over the phone," he said. "I'm going to be away selling all next week. I'll be back Saturday afternoon."

If he didn't make the team, it would be better if his mother told his dad over the phone. If he did make it, Eddie could tell him about playing goalie next Saturday. "Gee that's . . ." Eddie almost said "great," but caught himself in time.

"How about depressing?" his father asked. "Will that word do?"

"It will do fine." Eddie said with relief.

On Monday afternoon all the boys came over to the MacDougals' cellar with the excuse that they would work out. The only exercise they really got, though, was **running** up the stairs to see if the paper had arrived. Finally it came.

"We all made it!" Bud yelled. "I am playing for Olds Trucking, Archie for Thompsons Bakery and Eddie for Swangers Hardware."

"What's the next move, Mr. Trucking?" Eddie asked.

"Sit tight until Saturday's practice. Lucky you. The sponsor will give you goalie pads and a stick. All you'll have to furnish is your skates, although you should have them filed differently for goalie. Why don't you get your dad to do the job?"

"He's away at the moment, but I'll ask him when he gets back." To himself he said, "As soon as I tell him I made goalie." The boys left and Eddie went and told his mom that he had made the team.

"Wonderful," she said. "It will be nice to have another forward in the family. Your dad will be pleased."

Eddie realized he should tell his mother

that he had made goalie. But then she would tell his dad. It was up to him to break the news, and in person. "I've torn the clipping out for my scrapbook."

Saturday's practice went fine. The first part of the morning all the forwards, centers, defense and goalies worked separately.

Chuck Ives, the Blues' regular goalie, told them, "The goalie should have special skates, but you can get by with your regular skates if you have them rounded off at the ends. This will enable you to turn and stop very quickly. Don't keep your skates too sharp. A good way to take the edge off them is to run them across your stick. You're more interested in moving sideways than in moving forward."

Eddie dulled his skates. The rounding would have to be done later. After he had told his dad. They had two games with two periods of five minutes each. Eddie played goalie one of the periods and had a shutout. Goalie was fun to play. Eddie was getting to like it more and more.

"A week from this coming Friday night will be the jamboree," Speed said, after calling a halt. "There will be six periods of ten minutes each. Each team will play against another team for one period. It is a preview for you and your parents and friends to see what the teams will look like. This year we are going to charge fifty cents admission. This will be used to help pay some of the expenses."

On the way home Bud said, "Gee, you're lucky. All you have to do is carry your skates."

"Oh, my gosh, I didn't think!" Eddie said. "Do me a favor. Let me borrow your stick

for today. I'll get back to you tomorrow, I promise."

"Sure, but what's the story?"

Eddie couldn't tell him that to walk in his house without a stick would start a lot of questions. Why shouldn't a forward have a stick? "No questions, please," he said, as he took Bud's stick.

His father greeted him when he came in the door. "Congratulations. How did practice go? Did you score any goals?"

"Practice went fine but I didn't score."

"Settle down. I want to hear all about it. Who were the coaches? When's the first game?"

Now was the time to tell him, but Eddie hesitated. It was getting harder every day.

"Tomorrow would be better," he thought. He then told his dad all the details without telling a single lie. As he was talking, his dad picked up the skates from the floor.

"Holy smoke!" he said. "You must have done a lot of skating. These skates are as dull as one of my old razor blades." He ran his fingers over the edges. "It will take me all weekend to get them sharpened."

Eddie didn't say anything.

4. Fallacious Reasoning

Mr. MacDougal was home all that week, but Eddie didn't tell him about playing goalie. No time seemed just the right time. Coming home on the bus after Saturday's practice, Eddie thought, "I'll tell him today." But his dad wasn't home when he arrived. "I'll tell him at supper," he thought. But at supper something else happened.

"What in the world are you doing with your skates?" his dad asked. "I've sharpened them again. At this rate there will be nothing left of the blades. Are you walking on concrete?"

This would have been the perfect time to tell him; but his voice sounded a little angry, and Eddie only answered, "No." Then he remembered something else. "The jamboree is next Friday night. Will you be able to come?" If his dad said yes, then he would have to tell him now.

His dad pulled out his date book. "I'm sorry, son, but I won't be able to be there. I'm leaving Thursday on a trip and have an appointment Saturday morning. I won't be home until late Saturday afternoon."

"That's depressing, dad," Eddie said, trying to sound really sorry. Maybe if he could prove himself as a goalie it would be easier to tell his dad. But what if he was a flop? Friday's game would be the first test.

Thursday night his dad called. "His Saturday appointment has been canceled," his mother said. "He is going to drive home Friday night and come straight to the arena. Aren't you excited?"

"Holy smoke! I'll say I'm excited. I'm..." Eddie didn't finish the sentence. "I'm going downstairs, Mom, and work out."

He picked up a bar bell and brought it up to his waist. Why hadn't he told his dad? He stood there, forgetting that he still had the bar bell in his hands. Finally the weight brought him back to reality and he put it back on the floor. He got on the bike. "Holy smoke!" he cried. "What about my skates?"

Since he hadn't told his dad about goalie, he couldn't ask him to round off the ends. Swangers Hardware had done the job. What would his dad say to that? As if things weren't bad enough anyway. He pedaled furiously for a few minutes and then went upstairs. By Friday night he was a nervous wreck.

"It looks like we're all here," Speed Randall said as he looked around the dressing room. "A team will play a total of three

periods. One period against each team. Swangers Hardware against Olds Trucking will be the first. Remember, this is just for fun and not for the championship."

A burst of applause greeted the boys as they skated out. The arena looked entirely different now that it was filled with people and all the lights were on. Eddie tried to pick out his mother as he skated over to the goal. He finally saw her in the mezzanine. There was an empty seat beside her. His dad hadn't arrived yet. Then he had no more time to think about her, for the referees were coming on the ice. Eddie worked up slush in the crease. This was a good idea because it would slow down the puck. He needed all the help he could get.

Two of the Blues' regulars were going to be the referees. One of them skated to the center of the rink with the puck for the face-off. The whistle blew, and he dropped the puck. The Olds center took the puck and passed it to the right wing, Bob. Bob started his figure eight as he came toward Eddie and shot the puck toward the goal. Eddie automatically had moved to the right side of the cage and he blocked the shot easily. He passed it to one of his men as the crowd yelled. It was an easy save, but Eddie began to relax a little bit.

Ten minutes passed very quickly. The period ended 0-0; Eddie had made eight saves. Eddie sat on the bench and watched the other teams play. His team would play again next period. He found his mother again, and there still was an empty seat. Maybe his dad wouldn't arrive in time, and then he would have a chance to tell him. But as he skated out for the next game, he noticed a late arrival in the aisle, looking for his seat. It was his dad!

Eddie wasn't even aware of the faceoff. All he could think of was his dad sitting up in the stands. Why hadn't he told him earlier? The

next thing he knew the puck had sailed between his legs. He turned quickly around and saw the red light, and realized what had happened. The first time he had been scored on, and with his dad watching. "No more of that," Eddie said. "I'm going to be the best goalie here tonight."

Then someone from the crowd yelled, "Settle down, Eddie." He recognized his father's voice.

That was the only score for the other team —although there was one close call. The left forward of Thompsons Bakery shot to center who passed his stick over the puck instead of passing it to the right forward. He then shot the puck toward the goal. It was a beautiful fake and a beauty of a shot, for the puck left

the ice. Eddie caught it in his glove, and the crowd yelled with pleasure. Swangers Hardware won 2-1.

The rest of the evening went very fast. Eddie's team played one more time, but the other Swanger goalie played. That game ended 1-1. The Swanger team was a team that was going to be hard to beat.

When he came out of the locker room, his father and mother were waiting for him.

"I'm sorry I didn't tell you about playing goalie," Eddie said hurriedly. "I wanted to be a forward but I figured I was too slow, and my ankle broke sometimes when I skated too fast. I'm a better goalie. You're not disappointed in me?"

"Proud and disappointed. Proud because you're a good goalie. Disappointed because you didn't think you could tell me about it. But that shot through your legs told me you might have learned something about putting things off...."

Eddie interrupted, "It sure did! In fact," and he smiled, "you get an assist on that one."

"Here, let me take those skates. I understand now why they had to be so dull," Mr. MacDougal said. "You realize, of course, that your reasoning was...fallacious."

"Holy smoke! A goal!" Eddie said, and his mother and father both laughed. "Gee, everything's..." and he paused, trying to come up with the exact word.

"How about wonderful, marvelous, stupendous..." his mother said.

"All very fine, but I think I'll use a nickel word. Everything's swell."

F   10225
L   Lord, Beman

           Rough Ice

DATE DUE
